MARTY MOOSE GETS SICK

Written by
Kiki

Illustrated by
SOUSOU YERETSIAN

Published by
Montbec Inc.

Publisher
MATT ARENY

Publication Advisor
JOSE AZEVEDO

Editorial Supervisor
ETHEL SALTZMAN

Artwork Supervisor
PIERRE RENAUD

ISBN 2-89227-227-0

Chuck E. and his friends had never had any serious health problems. At their age, there was the occasional cold or sore throat, but never anything that kept them home from school for more than a few days. They had sometimes heard of other people having to go to the hospital because they were ill, but they never thought it would happen to one of them.

It was Monday morning, and the start of another school week. Everyone was standing outside of Chippy's house, waiting for the school bus. They were talking about the weekend and how much fun they had. Everyone except Marty. He was just standing around looking very quiet and solemn.

"Say, Marty, is there anything wrong?" Chuck E. asked with concern.

"No, it's just my throat," Marty explained in a raspy voice. "It's very sore, and I find it hard to talk."

"Oh, I'm sure it'll be okay," Chuck E. comforted his friend. "Just try not to talk too much."

"I'm trying not to," Marty said, "but what's going to happen when I get asked a question at school and I can't speak?"

"Well, that won't be so bad!" Chippy interrupted. "At least you'll have a good excuse!"

"I still think I'd rather have my voice back!" Marty rasped.

"Marty's right." Chuck E. added. "I'm sure you'd rather be healthy than not have to answer questions at school, Chippy. Nothing's more important than good health!"

"That's true," Gerty agreed. "I'm sure your throat will be just fine in a couple of days, Marty."

"Thanks, Gerty," Marty said. "You're a real friend!"

In a short while, the school bus stopped and picked them up. The day went by very quickly. When everyone was finally on board the school bus for the trip home, Chuck E. looked around to ask Marty how he was feeling, but Marty was nowhere in sight.

"Say, Gerty, where's Marty?" Chuck E. asked.

"Oh, he left early, after lunch," Gerty explained. "His parents came to pick him up. His voice and throat were getting worse as the day went on, so the teacher decided to call his parents to take him home."

"Gee, I hope he's okay!" Chuck E. said with concern. "I'll call his house tonight to see how he is."

"That's a good idea!" Gerty said. "If he's going to be away from school for a few days, I could bring him his homework."

"I think he'd really appreciate that!" Chippy remarked sarcastically. "That's all he needs, homework when he's sick!"

"Oh, Chippy, we're only trying to help," Chuck E. explained, "and we'd do a lot better if you'd help too, instead of joking around!"

"Okay, okay!" Chippy said. "What can I do?"

"Well, maybe you could take good notes, so that Marty could copy them while he's away. That way he won't fall too far behind," Chuck E. suggested.

"Oh, alright, I guess I can do that," Chippy agreed.

"And what can we do?" Skippy and Bobby asked.

"Well, you can come with us to visit him and cheer him up!" Chuck E. said.

"Okay!" Skippy and Bobby replied with enthusiasm.

"Gee, this sounds like a lot of trouble just for a sore throat," Chippy commented.

"Well, I'm sure you'd appreciate it, if you were sick and we helped you out," Gerty stated.

"You're right, I would," Chippy admitted. "But maybe Marty will be back tomorrow."

"Well, if he is, great!" Chuck E. said. "But if he isn't, then we'll be ready to help out."

After Chuck E. got home from school, he called Marty's house to see if he was okay. Mrs. Moose answered, and explained to Chuck E. that Marty's tonsils were infected and they had to come out. He would be going to the hospital in the morning for the operation, and he would be away from school for about a week.

"Oh, my!" Chuck E. replied with concern. "Will he be able to talk again?" he asked.

"Oh, yes," Mrs. Moose said happily. "Lots of kids have their tonsils taken out. In fact, mine were removed when I was Marty's age and, as you can hear, my voice is just fine!"

"Oh, I'm so glad!" Chuck E. said with relief. "But why does Marty have to have an operation?"

"Well, if he doesn't, he could keep getting very sore throats for a long time," Mrs. Moose answered. "I don't think he'd like that very much, do you?"

"I guess not," Chuck E. said. "Do you think we could all come and visit him in the hospital tomorrow?" he asked.

"I think he would really like that!" Mrs. Moose replied. "No one likes being sick, especially if you can't be with your friends. I think he'll feel a lot better if he knows you'll be visiting him."

"Thanks, Mrs. Moose!" Chuck E. said. "We'd really like to come!"

That night, Chuck E. told his parents about Marty and his operation, and asked if he and his friends could visit Marty after school. They agreed, as long as Mrs. Groundhog took them there and gave them a ride home. The next morning, Chuck E. told the rest of the gang about Marty, and asked Mrs. Groundhog if she wouldn't mind taking them to the hospital after school. Mrs. Groundhog said she would be happy to.

Chuck E. made sure that everyone knew what they had to do.

"Okay, Chuck E., I'll get all the homework for the day," Gerty said.

"And I'll take good notes." Chippy added.

"And we'll come with you to the hospital to help cheer Marty up." Skippy and Bobby said.

"Great!" Chuck E. exclaimed. "We'll make Marty forget about his sore throat!"

At lunch time, the rest of the gang got permission from their parents to go to the hospital after school. Through the day, Gerty gathered up all the homework for Marty, while Chippy took very good notes for Marty to use. They all gathered in Mrs. Groundhog's classroom after school, and they were soon on their way to the hospital.

When they arrived, Mrs. Groundhog checked with reception to find out which room Marty was in. Then they all got into the elevator, which took them to the third floor. As they walked along, in search of Marty's room, they came across Mr. and Mrs. Moose sitting in the hallway.

"Hi, Mr. and Mrs. Moose," Chuck E. greeted them. "How's Marty?"

"Oh, he's just fine, Chuck E.," Mrs. Moose smiled. "He's sleeping now. He's had quite a day," she explained.

"Yeah, I bet he has. Maybe the children should come back tomorrow instead," Mrs. Groundhog suggested.

"No, he's looking forward to this visit," Mrs. Moose replied. "I think he'd be very disappointed if he didn't get to see everyone. Maybe he's awake now. I'll go in and check."

Mrs. Moose went into Marty's room and
soon came out with a smile. She said that
Marty was awake and wanted everyone to
come in. The gang went inside and saw
Marty sitting in bed, looking very tired
but happy.

"Hi, Marty!" they said as they came up alongside of the bed. "How are you feeling?" Chuck E. asked.

"I-I'm okay," Marty replied with great difficulty.

"Now, don't try to say too much if it hurts," Chuck E. said. "We'll do the talking!"

"Okay, Chuck E.," Marty agreed, his voice sounding very strained and hoarse.

Chuck E. and the kids told Marty all about what happened at school that day, as well as how much everyone had missed him. This brought a big smile to Marty's face and a tear to his eye. He was very happy to see all of his friends, and grateful that they cared enough to come and see him when he was sick.

After a while, a nurse came into the room with a big stuffed clown in her arms for Marty. She explained that it was a gift from all of his friends at Little Forest School.

Marty was delighted. "Thanks, everyone!" he said with tears in his eyes, "I'll never forget this!"

"Oh, you're welcome, Marty!" Gerty said. "We all chipped in at school. We thought you'd like it!"

"I love it!" Marty's joy was greater than the pain in his throat.

Another nurse came in with a bowlful of ice cream. She told the gang that they would soon have to leave, so that Marty could get his rest.

"Say, Marty, why the ice cream?" Chippy asked.

"It's to help soothe my throat," Marty told him. "I can eat as much as I like."

"Wow!" Chippy exclaimed. "Maybe I should get my tonsils out!"

"I don't think you'd say that if you knew how much it hurts," the nurse tried to explain. "All the ice cream you could eat wouldn't make up for that."

Chippy thought it over. "Maybe you're right," he said.

"Believe me, she's right," Marty managed to say. "I know, and I wouldn't want to do it for all the ice cream in the world. But it sure helps having all of you here. I felt very frightened this morning, but now I feel much better!"

"Will you be coming by tomorrow?" he asked hopefully.

"We'll be here for sure," Chuck E. promised.

The gang stopped by the hospital every day after school, until Marty was well enough to go home. Once Marty was back in school, they asked him to show everyone the place where his tonsils had been. The operation was something he would never forget, and neither would his friends.

When a friend gets sick,

Show that you care.

Stop by and visit

With happiness to share!

Your friend,

Chuck E.